BETWEEN THE LINES

It was the onset of the hot and unbearably muggy season. If you had any hope of saving money on electricity, you knew you just had to tough it out and sleep with only the very lightest of blankets on at night. It was challenging, annoying, and almost virtually impossible. Tossing and turning became a nightmarish hell that you were awake for half of the time. And just when you'd slip off into something vaguely akin to blissful sleep, your body would shift automatically, contorting itself in search of the most comfortable position. You'd be awake all over again. The real shame was that you liked sleeping. Who didn't, honestly? But it left you groggy the next morning when the buzzer of your alarm—

Wait, had you set the alarm? You don't remember doing that. Or any reason for doing it. It's not like you had to be at work. When you half-consciously decided that, no, that wasn't your alarm, you realized it was the ring of the bell for the door downstairs. Someone was ringing your apartment. As you sat up, it only seemed to get louder and louder. It was impossible, it only had one setting, but the frequency lessened between each annoying chime. Eventually, you had to force yourself to the door at abounding speed. And even by then, your nerves were frayed.

You practically leaned against the button to the speaker. "What? Hello? What??" The miffed tone in your voice couldn't have been anything but very apparent.

"I need breakfast. Come get breakfast with me."

The ridiculousness of this statement- or demand, rather, was incredibly vexing. For one, you didn't have any friends in the area stupid enough to come proverbially bang on your apartment door for morning shenanigans. They all, mostly, knew that you were not and were never going to be a morning person. But secondly...

"Andy?"

The tone of his voice is what caught you off guard completely. In a reflexive movement, you jabbed the front door unlocked and slid the one to your own door open. Already you could hear him traipsing up the stairs as you stepped away from the entrance to sit back down on your bed. Once he was in, he didn't even bother locking the door, instead just bounding up to the foot of your bed. You were clearly in no mood, and nowhere even ready, to be outside at-

"Is it eight?" The symbols on your bedside clock remind you just how obnoxious Andy could be when he was around. But that was just it. Before he could even smile that dopey smile at you, "Why are you here at eight o'clock in the morning?"

Not just the unbelievable early hour, but why was he in the city at all? If he'd been planning on coming up, why hadn't he just called or texted a little in advance? Rubbing the sleep out of your eyes wasn't doing anything towards making you feel more awake.

"Give me a break. I'm on vacation." He came closer only so he could nudge your shoulder. "And I'm also starving. So let's go." As if you had no real choice in the matter-

Well. Really. You'd let him in, so now he wasn't going to go away until you got up. Your mistake. "Oh..."

Then the shaking began, both hands on your shoulders. "Come on." Whining was your least favorite thing that he did, mostly because it always worked. This time was no different, and you stood up to retrieve a pair of jeans, to push back your hair into slightly less of the morning mess that it was and grab your wallet and keys.

After that, you both went out the door and downstairs onto the newly warming sidewalk. The sun was up and a reminder of just how little you slept, so you let him lead the way. Thankfully he didn't go too far, and the diner was empty this early on a weekday morning. The waitress was not even there for three seconds before, "Coffee. Please." It was just above a beg. If there were any chance of getting through the day, you'd need a lot.

Whatever Andy ordered went right over your head- mostly because you weren't listening. But when the woman left, he turned his attention directly to you. "Not even one 'it's nice to see you?'" He was feigning injury, mostly because he absolutely knew that he was skirting the line of trouble.

"What are you doing here?" He had yet to answer that- well. Really answer it. "Or do I not want to know until after I've had my coffee?" Andy was spontaneous when he wanted to be but involving you in those sorts of plans was usually not a safe bet, for many reasons—of which he was intimately familiar with by now. Or at least he should have been.

"Vacation- thanks," The last part murmured to the waitress who set the two cups of steaming coffee down on the table before leaving. "Caught a red-eye and came up." The look on his face, that damnably cute little smile of his, was very proud. Andy kept a very hectic schedule. It was a surprise he had time to do anything else.

Then again…

You took two long sips of your hot, delicious morning beverage before you could think of speaking again. "Why here?" No. Wrong question— "Why me?" Andy loved the city. It was where he grew up, where you both grew up. Giving him less chance for going around in circles would be suitable for your frayed nerves.

But as he frowned at you, genuinely so, you thought maybe that was not an excellent question to have asked. "Why not you?"

"Am I being an ass?" Sometimes you weren't sure. It was harder around him because of the lengthiness of the jokes you shared and the blurred lines of everything else. When he only answered with the same expression, you waved your hand. "Alright. Sorry. Didn't get much sleep last night."

This cavalcade of nonsense had been going on for years, and both of you were too flighty and too busy to do anything more than dance around something more serious. Serious was bad, anyway. It had the chance to mar something that had probably been the best memories of your life. Losing those in favor of taking a shot in the dark was not the best idea. You knew he felt the same way.

It was worth putting up with random red-eye flights and Andy banging on the door for breakfast. And nights when you wished you were braver.

"It's okay." Smiling again, as easily as ever. The waitress stepped back over, and he ordered a ridiculous amount of food, half of which he probably wasn't going to eat. You tried something simpler, just for the sake of it. Fruit and some toast-...and, oh OK, maybe some eggs. "So, what do you want to do while I'm here?"

As if his entire 'vacation' plans revolved around you. But now that he'd said it that way, they probably did. Well. If you wanted to be involved. If you really couldn't, you knew he'd understand. "How long are you here for?" Probably the right place to start.

"I don't know yet." Just the easiness of this statement...

"You're the worst." Already he was set to a small giggle, one that threatened to coax a similar sound out of you, so you hid your smile behind your cup. He really was the worst. In the best way. "I don't know..." Making plans on the fly was not your forte. "We could go up to Coney." Or something equally as stupid.

"No beach." As if he really needed to remind you.

"You don't have to get in." Grinning at him and that mildly uncomfortably look on his face, the small furrow of his brows. Because he knew you knew better. "Oh, relax. There's other stuff to do up there." The boardwalk was nice. So was the park. And the aquarium was not too far... There probably weren't many places in the city that you and Andy hadn't been to at least twice already. So just throwing something out and just going- well. That's what he was good at. Still, after all this time, you had to try to be that efficient at on-the-fly.

"Okay. Sounds like a good day." There was little chance of things going awry with such little planned, but there was always that cloud that followed you around. At least he was familiar with it by now.

"I have to take a shower first. If I find you sleeping on the bed, I'm not waking you up." He'd probably slept on the flight up, but if he conked out, it was an easy excuse for you just to climb in next to him and sleep the night of tossing and turning off. "Subway should take like... an hour." It was the worst part of the day, no doubt, but once it was over, it was over. That is until you had to head back the other way.

"It's good- I have stuff I have to work on."

"I thought you said you were on vacation?" You phrased it in a particularly facetious way because he never stopped, even when he was supposed to. When he just rolled his eyes and turned his head away with a smile, you shook your head. "...it is nice to see you, by the way." A little softer than the rest of your conversation.

"I knew it." So entirely proud of himself.

"Oh, just shut up and eat your food." The waitress slid the plates across the table. The first round of fruit was shared between forks before you both went your separate ways back to your dishes. You tried not too hard to look at his face for too long or let his smile get to you too hard. This was always the most challenging part after long intervals of not having him around. But if you could just get through the morning…

***

Your shower was more or less of the short and sweet variety. Though it was always tempting to stick around in the hot water, even when the temperature outside could be nasty, you had a day planned. Aside from that, the more time you spent in, the more time you risked Andy falling asleep. Though he'd promised not to, there was a good chance. If you let that happen, there was also a much higher risk that you wouldn't be able to wake him up and would end up wasting the day sleeping next to him in a curled-up ball.

Yet though you tried to keep your time in short, when you got out, Andy was lying on your bed, legs over the edge, feet on the floor. His eyes seemed closed, but you couldn't see through that ever-growing thick fringe of shaggy brown hair. He could have sat on the couch or waited anywhere else that would have been out of the line of sight of a potentially naked you- but why would he do that?

On closer approach, you stood between his legs, and he tilted his head down, just enough for you to realize he hadn't been napping but merely staring up at the white emptiness of your ceiling. His hands slid up underneath him, easing a slow transition to half sitting upright, and you threw all notions of potentially ruining the day away as you moved to sit in his lap, legs on both sides of him. You let go of the clasp on your towel in favor of taking hold of both his shoulders to sustain your position.

He helped by sliding his hands to your hips. No words were passed between the two of you, only watching each other's eyes. Then you found it entirely impossible not to give in. Your hands moved up to the sides of his face before combing back through his hair, curling in at the base with a half-tight grip that got his eyes to go half-lidded and a breathy hot puff of air to leave his lips in a shiver. "When are you going to cut this mop?" With anyone else, this would be at risk for ruining the mood.

But he took it in stride, a dazed smile on his lips. "What, you don't like it?" That was hardly the case, but every time one of you made it to the other side of the country, it just got longer and longer. Instead of answering, you leaned down into him, coaxed by the upward movement of his hands along your back. His lips met yours in a sweet kiss, and it wasn't long before his tongue twined around yours. When you both broke back, "I thought about this like a million times on the plane."

This drew a soft, if not entirely knowing, laugh out of you. "I bet you did. Pervert."

Andy's laugh wasn't too far off, a soft rumble of that infectious noise that warmed your heart. "Not like that." To this, you only teased him further with an 'mm hmmm,' so he leaned back to get a better look at you. "I'm serious." Thinking about this took a little too long for his liking, "I mean—"

Risking letting him talk his way around his feelings any further was a bad idea. So you silenced him with another tug of his hair and a kiss. The sound in the back of his throat was just as grateful as it was warm and needy. It didn't last long. By the time he was pulling back, he was also making the switch to lie you on the bed.

Then his lips found a slow and steady trail along your jawline and then to your neck. A careful graze of his teeth followed a brush of the stubble of his chin.

Then you risked things, too. "I think about you probably just as much." The sex, too, because it was never worth not thinking about. But when he wasn't around, there was no reason to lie and say you didn't miss him. "—but you could have told me you were coming."

The laugh from his lips vibrated along your chest as he was still moving, peeling back your towel inch by inch. "You can't still be mad." As if he knew you weren't. And he was right. Before you had time to deny it in a playful lie, his lips found the peak of your breast, a gentle tug of his lips followed by an even more delicate play with his teeth.

A betrayal left your lips in the form of a wordless moan and your hips, still half-hidden, shifted up to meet his. "I can if you don't hurry up." Putting yourself through the song and dance that was Andy's lovemaking was worth it more often than not. But the time apart was too much, and now that he'd started, you couldn't help but be hungry.

Even he had a small question about it, leaning back up to run his lips teasingly against yours, watching your eyes with his. "You don't want—?" Curious, too, that after the time apart, you wouldn't want to spend it slowly.

Explorative, and he'd be good for it, too.

But impatience was one of your key traits. "I do." A little needier than you meant. He already knew he held most of the cards, even if he never in his life used them against you in a harmful way. Admitting it was hard, though. "But not right now." Right now, there was only one thing you did want.

His laugh was kind and just short of a murmur. "I'll hold you to that." The tone in which he promised such things sent a tremble through your entire body. Something he was smart enough to pick up on. But when you grasped at his hair again, he lost his sense of control, and his hands were moving between the two of you to unhitch his belt and edge his pants down just enough.

One of your hands went down, fingers skirting his cock. Feeling how hard he was already. How much he wanted just as badly as you did. Then you shifted the towel back all the way and hooked one leg around his hips. His lips pressed together in the form of pseudo-concentration, one arm going underneath your back to hold you close as he edged into you inch by inch.

"Oh— Andy—"This was one of the things you thought about the most. Every last part of his thick cock sliding into your body. The noise that fell from his lips, the way his eyes rolled back as he couldn't keep it up any longer.

"Marian—"How easily he could lose his sense of self to your body, just as you could to his. And the terrible way he said your name just before cursing in nothing more than a breathy hitched whimper. It drove you crazy—every part of you.

He held you close with one arm and kept a tight grip with his other hand on your hip, fingers digging deep into your skin. Both your arms locked around his neck, and the next time you moaned, he dove down to take your mouth against his in a heated kiss. He swallowed everything you let go of after that. Every shift of your hips was met with formidable force back from his. Every time he pulled back out, you could just barely wait for him to slam back into your body. It devolved into senseless sex, but it was what you needed. What he wanted, too, after so long apart.

Later you'd take it slow. But just then, Andy pounding you hard into the mattress was worth the sleepless night, worth him being gone for so long.

"Andy," Nothing more than a quiver as you lost the energy to keep up with his frantic and rough rhythm.

His lips dropped, nuzzling the erratic pulse in your neck. He mumbled something back, but you couldn't hear what it was, not over the sound that fell from your lips as his teeth bit down hard into the crook of your neck after.

"Oh god!" It was about as much warning as he would get, not that he ever needed it. He knew the ins and outs of your body. I knew exactly what it took to push you to the edge and then pull you right over it. You felt his cock deep inside of you as he came, felt the way it twitched in response to your orgasm.

"Marian," Huffed out close to your ear, "Oh!" Your eyes rolled back as you listened to him lose it. You felt him lose it as he gripped both your hips to pull you into a hard thrust of his own, felt him come inside you, hot and heavy- a little dizzy from both your efforts. He moved a few more times after that, settling both of you through the throes before kneeling back, hands going to the mattress on both sides of your head.

He nudged your lips with his own, something affectionate and sweet, breathing hard in every other beat. When you managed a small flutter open of your eyes, you caught the lazy smile pointed in your direction. It had been so hard for so long not to fall in love with that face, but you'd stopped fighting a very long while ago.

"That's what you thought of, hm?" You were going back to teasing, though your tone was airy.

"A few other ways, but basically, yeah." A little choppy as his brain fumbled to form back from the mush it had turned into.

"Me too." The moment you said those two little words, his grin grew a little wider. So you attempted to shut up his non-verbal know-it-all smile with another kiss. It worked for about as long as it went on, but when it was over, he was moving away to lie down beside you.

"I think I'm ready for a nap. Are you ready for a nap?" The half-chuckle in his tone belied his real intentions.

But that didn't stop you from shoving his side before sitting up. "Don't even start with that crap." The day had just barely begun, and you were keen to see it through to its end, even if you knew you had to stay sitting to avoid the shakiness in your legs a little while longer.

***

The station wasn't too far, and luckily one of the nice trains pulled up instead of the older brand. You had to swipe Andy in with your metro card, but he promised to pay you back. It didn't matter since he'd picked up the check for breakfast- as he should have, anyway, since he basically dragged you out of your apartment at an ungodly hour in the first place. Inside it was cool and mostly empty in the car, and you both took the two-seater in the rear and settled in. The newer cars were good for watching the stops fly by on the electronic screens on the sides of the vehicle. Very useful for when you had your headphones in.

It was the first thing you went for as he pulled a pocket notebook out of his jeans and a small pencil to match. Ever the hard worker. "You mind?" It was likely you were going to fall asleep anyway- not that you would ever do that on your own, but you were still tired (not having slept, a full stomach, and good sex would do that to a person), and Andy would watch out for you. But of course, he had to make sure that drifting off to work on whatever it was he had in his head was okay.

You ended up drifting. It was just too much for you not to. But it ended sooner than you would have liked as he was shaking you. "Come on, sleepyhead, we're going to miss the stop."

There weren't enough grumbles in the known world to voice your real displeasure, but before you could have your say, he was pushing you so he could get up. Then he grabbed your arm and pulled you up and through the door. It was just in time, too, as some people were getting into the train from the platform, and then the doors closed behind. His notebook and pencil went back into his pocket, as did your headphones into yours, and you stretched. Luckily the station wasn't that close to the outside, no threatening mention from the sun.

"Where to?" The both of you hadn't planned the day too hard.

"Aquarium." But you had at least decided on that. The atmosphere would be friendly and calm and relaxed- less time to wander around the boardwalk while the sun was high and get burned. Coney would be next, and maybe you'd brave a few rides with him, but it wasn't for sure.

Andy just gave a firm nod, and without putting any thought into it, his hand slipped into yours, fingers locking, and you both walked out of the terminal and down the street. The entrance wasn't too far off, and you picked the ticket tab up, and in the both of you went. It was as dark as you remembered, the glass windows surrounding the two of you as you walked. There wasn't much conversation besides banal 'look at this' and 'over here.'

Though you didn't visit often, it was perhaps one of your favorite places. The moment you thought you'd wandered off to one of the big fish tanks and lost him, Andy put his arms around your waist from behind and pulled you to him. There still had yet to be any real discussion of why he'd blown off everything else and shown up. But you both already knew the reason for it. At the very least, you didn't want to talk about it.

But you got the feeling that he did. It made you nervous. Maybe the aquarium had been a low place to pick, with so much on his mind. At least if you were on a roller coaster or taking the go-karts around the track, there wouldn't have been any risk of…

His head leaned down on top of yours, the blue backlights of the tank reflecting across your faces. "Don't do it." You half begged him as a sigh escaped his lips.

"I can't." All the teasing and playing around you two had done, and there was no trace in his voice now. He sounded exactly like he'd said- he'd been thinking about you on the entire plane ride over, and probably for a lot longer than that.

There were a lot of problems with this, even though you were just as bad. "Why now?" It wasn't like the two of you had never tried to have this conversation, but it just never ended up well. It wasn't in the cards for the both of you. He was busy and lived on the other side of the county, and little surprise visits were great. Memories were great. But other than that, there wasn't much.

"I'm at a point…" He started, but there was a slight waver in his voice as his hands came tighter around you. As much as he'd thought about it, it seemed like he hadn't considered what to say. "Look— I'm at a point in my life where things are kind of how I want them to be." Doubling back before making it work aloud.

This was good, too. You were happy for him. No one deserved success as Andy did. He'd worked so hard for so long. He was too good not to have it. It was all you'd ever really wanted for him.

You stayed silent in an effort not to jump too far ahead or say anything you'd regret. Or worse yet, let his needs pull you far enough to a point where there was no going back. So he continued. "I'm doing things I love, and it's good." Your eyes lowered, watching one of the lankier fish swim about in circles near the bottom of the tank. "But you're the loose end."

The way he said it was like a punch in the gut, even though you knew there was no way he meant it negatively. Maybe it was just your penchant for pessimism, but that sounded like a goodbye. Things are great, so I'm calling a wrap- but that wasn't it. And it was just your sense of self trying to protect itself. Of course, Andy didn't mean this in any way save good, but getting angry could easily mean pushing him away and not dealing with it. Which, while it wasn't the best option, was the easiest.

You pushed half away from him, bracing up against the railing in front of the tank and looking up at him. His expression was hard to read, mostly because he was trying to do the same to yours. "What do you want me to do?" This wasn't a good question to ask because while he was stumbling, there was no doubt he did have a few answers for you. "Go home with you? Give up my apartment and the city and all my stuff? Call it quits for something we know that—"

It won't work. It isn't a good idea.

"Hey," In that soft warning tone that you only had ever heard him use. No one spoke it as good as he did- careful and able to stop you cold. "I would never ask you to do anything that would hurt you." There was a lingering here, and when you tilted your head away, "anything I didn't think you don't want."

Things between you and him were rarely ever this serious. That was just because it was far, far more comfortable to sit around and have a few drinks. Fuck occasionally. Meet when it was convenient, which was rare— and increasingly more so as the months went by, as his career took off, he was losing the time, becoming engrossed in the things he'd worked so hard for. And you were happy to let him because that was simpler. Looking up at his face, the water casting a pale white against him, illuminating the amber of his eyes.

The look of despair, too. He was making a big bet here. Because if you said no, you two would pretend things were okay. Carry on. And then when it was over, this little random vacation that no longer seemed like a vacation and more like a simple plan, you'd probably just never talk again. He was about to ruin things. Or risk ruining them. And for what?

"Andy..." You wished he hadn't. You hoped he hadn't come up to the city. Hadn't rung your doorbell. You wished you'd been so deeply asleep that you hadn't been able to answer it.

But most of all, you wished he wasn't right.

His eyes narrowed in a completely inquisitive way as he still searched your face. "Am I wrong?" The form he asked implied like he wasn't sure—and that frightened him. The big play he'd made, thinking it would be OK once it was over, it might not pan out. The realization that he was about to blow up years worth of this long not-relationship, once the thought swept over him, took his expression from unsure to devastated. "Forget it. Forget I said anything." So quickly as he held both his hands up in a gesture of surrender.

He had been willing to risk things when he believed he was right, but in the face of losing them to being wrong, he just couldn't handle it.

"I don't want to be your 'loose end.'" That felt extremely offensive. He was right where he wanted to be- well, almost, if it weren't for little ol' you. How terrible was that?

"Forget it," He'd started whining. "Please, Marian, please forget it." Begging, even.

You stepped forward, close enough for him to have to angle his head down to still look into your eyes. "Giving up?"

This confused him. "No, I just—"Now, in the face of having the thing he wanted but seemed like it was blowing apart, he didn't know what to do. This wasn't an enjoyable game to be playing for either of you. Worse yet, neither of you was skilled. Because this just wasn't part of what you two did. So, he sighed, shoulders dropped. "Yes or no?"

"It's not that simple." You thought being honest would help him out, but that only made it worse.

Much, much worse. "Come on, Marian. I can't do this little twisty dance with you. My heart can't handle it. I'm way too tired. And I just-"

You silenced him by reaching up with both hands, resting them on both of his shoulders, and pulling him closer. Instinctively his hands went to your hips, and he hushed, but the frown was evident on his lips. "I can't just drop everything and get on a plane with you." There was just no way. While in the land of fantasy, that might have been nice, it wasn't feasible. "But if this is what you want, I can look into it." Letting your apartment go back up and boxing all your things and-

Were you considering dropping everything you knew to find something with him? Andy, of all people?

"It's not about what I want." He seemed entirely dissatisfied with this answer. "Not entirely." That would be a colossal lie. Especially when he'd said how long he'd been thinking about this and how he wanted to finish this one significant chapter of his 'unfinished life' and move into something better. "What do you want?" His hesitancy as he asked this was clear as day, even if in the darkness of the aquarium, you couldn't see the more refined features of his face. But before you could say anything- "And don't give me some fake answer. I need you to be serious. I know you can."

If he wasn't so ready to vomit with anxiety, this could have been a tease or at least a small joke. But there was nothing about it for you to smile at. "We've been doing this for so long-"It might have picked up steam.

But he interrupted you with a very soft warning growl, "Marian." Clearly worried you were about to, as he called it, do some twisty dance around your feelings.

"Yes, okay? Yes, I'd like something a little more than 'oh look at me, I'm on random vacation let's fuck'." You're imitating his voice a few octaves lower and with a stupid drawl. Not that he sounded anything like that, but to be fair, he was just as frustrating at times.

There was a few beats of silence between you before, finally, thank god, he smiled. Relieved. "I said it wasn't just about the sex." Eventually, he'd edged back into territory more familiar to the both of you.

"Well. I just assume that's why you want me closer at hand." It wasn't - at all. This little thing you two had been doing for years was much more than that. And if you were brave enough, you might have called it love. But you weren't. He leaned in, pressing you to the railing protecting the glass, his hands sliding up the length of your body to take your face. "I'd be lying if I said it wouldn't be nicer to have you around." Moving close enough to kiss, but not ready, smirking just a little then. "For the- you know- the sex."

"Oh yes, I think I know." You'd only just been doing precisely that an hour ago.

He closed the gap, kissing you just once. It was soft, just a mixture of relief and promise. He pulled back, "So, did this whole little show I planned out work?" As if he had to ask after you'd said yes. But there was a little more reason to why he was saying it- giving a little bit of lightness back to the situation that was closing a significant chapter on both your lives and opening something a little bit scarier.

"Yeah, yeah," You drew out, as if entirely unimpressed with his antics. But it had taken a lot of guts. Now you really couldn't imagine how long and painful that flight over had been if this was what he'd been rehearsing for hours above the skies. "You win."

"Andy wins!" Self-deprecating humor was often your favorite, and this one got a good little giggle out of you- which he soon followed in as he took you back into his arms for a small but reassuring kiss. It was going to be alright, something in you said.